The Police Dog

Lady

Princess

Tramp

Our Hero, Scamp

SCHOLASTIC INC.

New York   Toronto   London   Auckland   Sydney
Mexico City   New Delhi   Hong Kong   Buenos Aires

"Be careful, Scamp!" Lady called, as she watched her son dash across the yard. "Don't bounce the ball too hard."

"All right!" the grey puppy answered. Scamp bounced the ball to his sisters. "Catch!" he shouted.

The sisters liked playing ball in the garden. It was fun, safe, and they never got dirty.

But Scamp grew tired of the game. "Can we go to the park?" he asked his father, Tramp.

"I can't take you today," Tramp replied.

"Can I go by myself?" Scamp asked.

Tramp had lived on the streets before he had met Lady. He understood how his son felt. And the park wasn't very far away. . . .

"All right," said Tramp finally. "You can go for a quick run in the park. But don't go anywhere else."

"I won't!" promised Scamp.

Scamp bounded out of the yard and into the street. There was so much to see! He stopped to watch two cars honking and beeping at one another. He thought about chasing the cars, but he remembered his promise to his father.

So Scamp continued down the street to the park. But as he passed an alley, he heard someone call for help!

Scamp peeked down the alley. He saw a pack of large dogs snarling at a little white puppy. The frightened puppy was backed up against a fence. She couldn't escape!

Brave Scamp knew he had to help her. But how? He certainly couldn't fight the other dogs the way his father could. Then Scamp had an idea.

Scamp carefully crept behind a trash can and pushed it over. CLANG! CLUNK! CRASH!

His trick worked. The noise frightened the big dogs away.

Unfortunately, Scamp had also made a big mess. Empty tin cans, apple cores, and even a black mask and some gloves were spread all over the ground.

But Scamp couldn't worry about a mess at the moment. He turned to the fluffy poodle, who was shivering with fear. "Don't be frightened!" Scamp said. "I'm your friend!"

The poodle smiled at Scamp. "Thanks. My name
is Princess," she said. "And you're my hero!"

Scamp liked being someone's hero! "Why were
those dogs bothering you?" asked Scamp.

"Because they wanted this," said Princess,
pulling something out from behind a box.

"Wow!" Scamp's eyes widened. In front of him
was the biggest bone that he had ever seen!

"Would you like to share it with me?" Princess offered generously.

"Sure!" Scamp replied, licking his lips. "I haven't had dinner yet."

But before they could taste the delicious-looking bone, the two puppies were startled by a sudden noise. Someone was coming down the alley!

"Those horrible dogs must be coming back!" Princess whispered.

"Quick, hide!" ordered Scamp. The two puppies huddled behind some boxes as the noise grew louder.

Scamp promised, "No matter what happens, I'll protect you, Princess!"

Then he peeked over the box to see what was causing the noise. It wasn't the dogs at all . . .

. . . It was the police! Princess was relieved, but Scamp was worried. The police were looking at the mess he had made in the alley.

Scamp was afraid that he and Princess would be taken to the dog pound if the police caught them. His parents would be angry. And they wouldn't trust Scamp to go out on his own again.

"C'mon," Scamp whispered to Princess. "Let's go."

While the police were busy examining the black mask and gloves, the two dogs sneaked away with the big bone. As soon as they were out of the alley, they began to run.

Scamp and Princess raced down a steep hill. It was hard for Scamp to run with such a huge bone— it felt heavier and heavier with every step. Finally, he had to drop the heavy bone. It landed on a manhole cover. Suddenly a worker opened the manhole cover from below. The bone began to roll down the hill!

Scamp quickly retrieved the bone. Then he thought about his promise to his parents. "Let's go to the park. It should be safe there!" Scamp said to Princess.

When they got to the park, Scamp put the bone down in a big pile of leaves. "Let's have a drink from the pond before we eat this," Scamp said. "The bone will be safe here."

But when they got back, Scamp saw that it had been swept away by the gardener, who was raking up leaves!

Scamp sprang into action. "Give it back!" he barked.

Scamp dived straight into the pile of leaves. "I know it's in here somewhere!" Scamp growled. The leaves tickled his nose as he searched the pile trying to find the bone.

"Hey, stop that!" the gardener scolded.

But before the gardener could grab him, Scamp had found the bone. He and Princess raced away once again.

They ran back to the street. "I'm never putting this down again," said Scamp. "I . . . ah . . . ah . . . ah-choo!"

The bone went flying through the air!

"Bless you!" said Princess, as she watched the bone sail straight through the open doors of a waiting bus.

"Stop!" Scamp barked at the bus. But the bus closed its door in his face and drove away. By now, Scamp had forgotten all about his promise to his parents. He just wanted to get Princess's bone back. The two dogs ran behind the bus, yapping as loudly as they could. "Woof! Woof! Woof!" they called.

When the bus stopped, Scamp jumped onboard.
The bus driver held out his hand. "Could I have
your fare, please?" he asked Scamp politely.

The passengers laughed but Scamp didn't care.
He quickly grabbed the big bone and leapt off the
bus before it drove away again. Scamp and Princess
once again headed for the park.

"At last, we can eat this bone," Princess said. But
she had spoken too soon. For not too far away,
Scamp spotted . . .

. . . a stern-looking police dog! He seemed to be looking for something. "Maybe he's looking for us because of the mess I made in the alley. Let's get out of here!" Scamp whispered urgently to Princess.

Scamp and Princess ran
to the other side of the park.
Unfortunately, the big dogs that had chased Princess
earlier were there! And they still wanted the bone.

"Run!" shouted Princess. But as
Scamp tried to get the huge bone through
a gate, it got stuck! Scamp was trapped!

Scamp closed his eyes. He was sure the big dogs were going to get the bone. But when he opened them, the big dogs had left. Instead, the police dog was towering over him!

"What's going on here!" demanded the police dog.

Meanwhile, back at the house, Lady and Tramp were worried because Scamp had been gone for so long. "He should have been home by now!" said Lady, looking troubled as she peered out of the gate.

"I think we should go out and look for him," Tramp decided firmly. He hoped that his son wasn't in any trouble.

But trouble was exactly what Scamp thought he was in. The puppy knew that he must tell the police dog the truth. "I made all that mess in the alley," Scamp confessed courageously.

"But he did it for a good reason," insisted Princess, standing up for her friend. "He did it to save me!" Then she added, "And my bone."

"Hmmm!" said the police dog gruffly. "Kindly stand back and allow me to examine the evidence."

The police dog sniffed and inspected every inch of the big bone. "Yes, I think this is it!" he announced. He could see that Scamp and Princess were confused. "Let me explain," he began.

"Last night there was a robbery at the museum," the police dog said. "A witness to the crime has told the police that the thief wore gloves and a black mask."

"I saw gloves and a mask!" Scamp said excitedly. "That's what the police were looking at today!"

"But what did the thief take?" wondered Princess.

"Recently, the museum obtained a complete dinosaur skeleton. The thief broke into the display room . . .

. . . and stole a priceless dinosaur bone," the police
dog finished.

"Just like our bone!" said Princess, trying to be
helpful.

"Exactly like your bone!" growled the police
dog. "Where did you get it?" he quizzed them.

Princess was cross that the police dog thought they might be the thieves. "I didn't steal it!" insisted Princess, as she stamped her paw adamantly. "I found it in the alley!"

"Maybe the real thief hid it there!" added Scamp.

The police dog looked at the two puppies. "Please come with me!" he barked.

At that moment, Lady and Tramp were looking anxiously for Scamp out on the busy streets.

Lady and Tramp searched the park . . . but Scamp wasn't there!

Then they went to the pond where Scamp loved to chase the ducks . . . but Scamp wasn't there.

They even went to Tony's restaurant . . . but
Scamp wasn't there, either!

Lady burst into tears. "Oh, where can our Scamp
be?" she sobbed.

Tramp knew that there was only one place left to look—the dog pound!

Together, the two dogs headed for the dog pound. "I just hope Scamp isn't in any trouble!" Lady whispered.

DOG POUND

But before they entered the dog pound, they
heard someone shout, "Scamp!"

Tramp froze in his tracks. "What's that?!" he
wondered.

They saw a crowd of excited people at the
museum down the street. They heard someone call to
Scamp again.

"Our Scamp!" Lady cried, as she and Tramp
tried to push their way through the crowd!

Lady and Tramp soon spotted their son.

Tramp was puzzled. "What's Scamp doing at the museum?"

"And with a police dog by his side!" said Lady. Now she was really worried that he might be in trouble.

Scamp saw his parents and raced over to them. "I'm so happy to see you!" he said, laughing.

"What's going on here?" Tramp wondered.

Scamp said, "I can explain everything. But first, I want you to meet my new friend, Princess."

"Your son's a hero. He saved me!" Princess told them.

Lady smiled at Princess and turned to Scamp. "But why didn't you come home from the park?"

"I'm sorry I broke my promise," Scamp apologized. "But I had to help the police clear up a robbery first!"

Lady and Tramp watched as people took photos
of Scamp, Princess, and the big bone!

"Oh, I'm so proud that our son has helped the police," said Lady.

"Proud?" answered Tramp truthfully. "I'm amazed! Our Scamp isn't a troublemaker—our Scamp is a hero!"

Suddenly the head of the museum announced loudly, "And now, our heroes will put the stolen bone back where it belongs!"

Scamp and Princess put the bone in exactly the right spot. It fit the dinosaur skeleton perfectly! "It's just like putting the last piece in a giant jigsaw puzzle!" Scamp said, chuckling.

"And to thank our little heroes, we've prepared a little feast." The head of the museum motioned to a long table with a flourish.

Scamp licked his lips. He had never seen so much delicious food all at once. And at last there were stacks of bones for him and Princess to eat!

"Yum, yum!" Scamp shouted joyfully. "Bone appetit!"

Scamp, Princess, and everyone else quickly dug
in to the incredible banquet. "This more than makes
up for the big bone that we didn't get to eat," said
Princess gratefully.

Scamp was thrilled that he was able to help the police and the museum . . . and also that he had made a new friend, Princess!